Don't Kiss the Frog!

KINGFISHER

First published 2008 by Kingfisher
an imprint of Macmillan Children's Books
a division of Macmillan Publishers Limited
20 New Wharf Road, London N1 9RR
Basingstoke and Oxford
Associated companies throughout the world
www.panmacmillan.com

ISBN: 978-0-7534-1304-3

Don't Kiss the Frog!

Princess Stories with Attitude

Chosen by Fiona Waters

KINGFISHER

For *Princess Daisy May*
with much love from
Fiona

Contents

Introduction

"Once upon a time . . .
and they all lived HAPPILY EVER AFTER."

These spellbinding words open and close the door to that far-off land where magic and enchantment reign – but also where boringly good behaviour is always rewarded, rose-tinted glasses are firmly in place and princesses are usually simpering nincompoops, unable to think beyond the next party frock before being married off to some impossibly handsome prince.

Yet some frogs resolutely remain frogs, despite all attempts to kiss them into human form, and in this collection absolutely no one simpers – except the occasional weedy Royal Poet. Princess Rose, whose best friend Rapunzel would like to cut her hair short and dye it blue, wants a prince who is kind to animals and likes chocolate; Princess Wendy turns down her frog-prince because he smells – fine in a frog, but not so attractive in a prince; Princess Jane thinks that she might like to be a conventional frilly-dress-marble-palace-glittery-tiara kind of princess, but soon finds that all that sparkles is not necessarily satisfying; Princess

6

Grace is so clumsy she trips over her dress's train with embarrassing regularity; Sleepy Beauty can hardly wake up, even for tea. And then there is the dragon, who loses his fire in a most humiliating manner, but then discovers an enterprising way to regain his composure.

The writers here have their tongues very firmly in their cheeks, and nothing is more delightful for young readers than a whiff of anarchy. Classic fairytales such as the timeless treasures of the Brothers Grimm, Hans Christian Andersen and Charles Perrault are central to a child's literary heritage, but these princess tales take a different approach. A good helping of disrespect has produced a collection of brilliant and lively stories that will delight and entertain all readers – *princesses*, dragons and frogs alike.

Fiona Waters

The Clumsy Princess

Lou Kuenzler

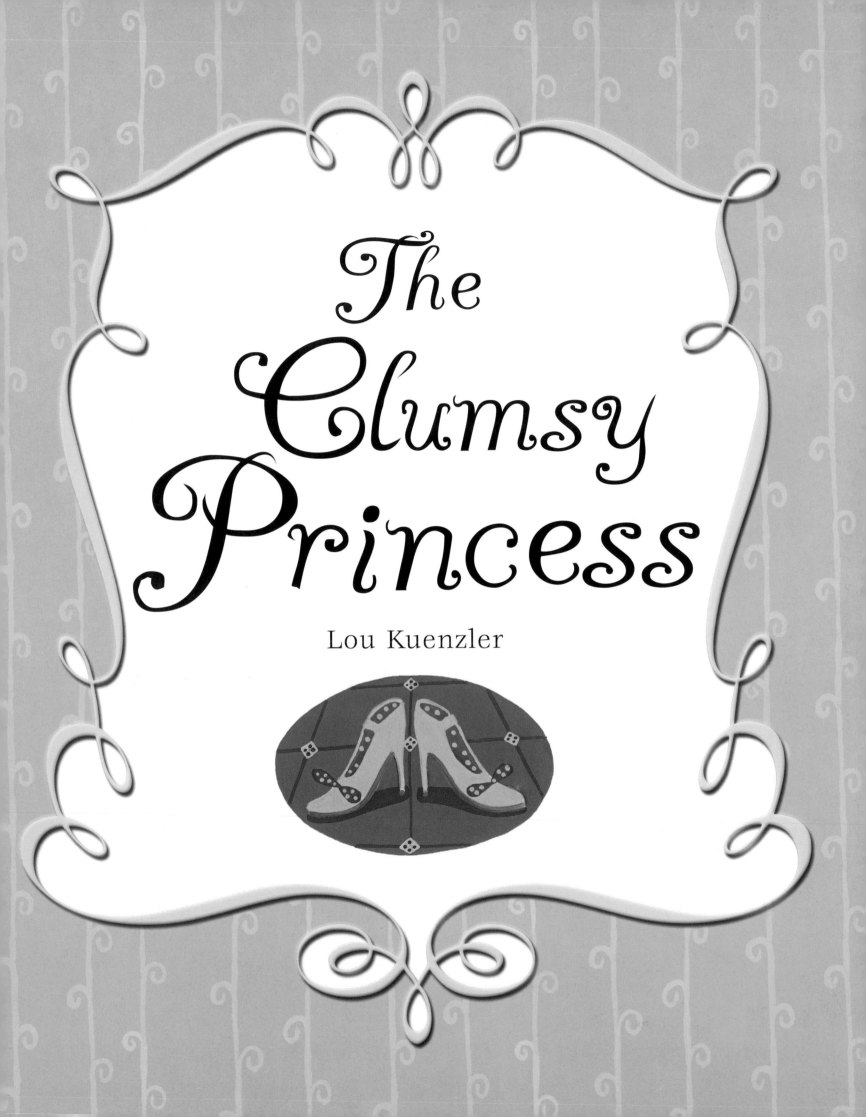

There
was once a
princess
named
Grace.

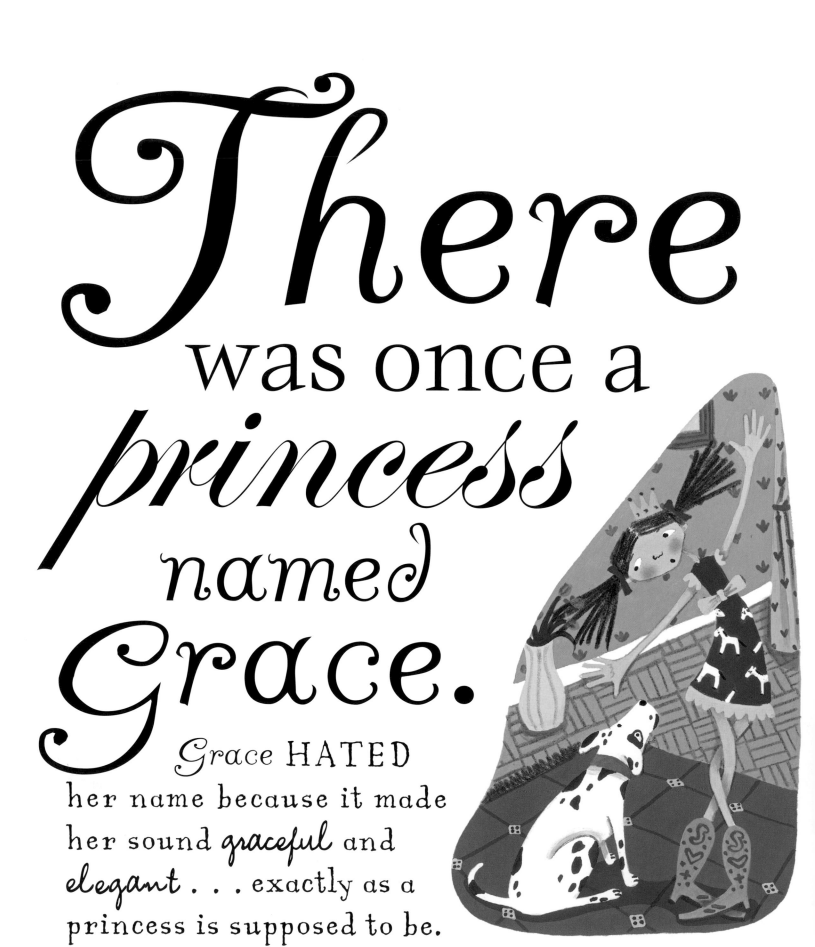

Grace HATED
her name because it made
her sound *graceful* and
elegant . . . exactly as a
princess is supposed to be.

But Grace was not graceful or elegant. Grace was TALL and spindly with very BIG feet. She had l-o-n-g legs like strands of spaghetti, which – just like spaghetti – spent most of their time tangled up. Grace was always falling over, knocking things down and tripping up.

One morning, as she fell downstairs for breakfast, Grace found that the castle had been hung with scarlet banners. A GRAND TOURNAMENT was to be held – a jousting competition at which every knight in the kingdom would have the chance to prove his skill.

"Grace must curtsey to the winning knight and present him with a handkerchief," declared the king.

"OH NO!" wailed Grace. "The last time I tried to curtsey, my knees got knotted together. I fell over and knocked poor Sir Splashalot into the moat."

"You'll just have to practise," said the king.

Grace stuck out her bottom and tried to look elegant. Bump! Her backside collided with a servant carrying a great big pot of porridge. With a sticky splash he tumbled headfirst into the gooey pot, his legs sticking out like spoons.

"S-s-sorry," stammered Grace.

"Come on," the queen said with a sigh. "It's time to have a fitting for the dress you will wear."

The dress was gold and shiny and as l-o-n-g as a cathedral aisle.

"Don't trip on the hem," warned the queen.

Grace's stomach churned like a water wheel.

"Can't I ride my pony?" she begged. "The winning knight will be on his horse. I can present the hankie like that."

Grace loved to ride. It was the only time she didn't feel clumsy. If her pony's legs did the walking for her, Grace wouldn't trip and fall.

"RIDE?" shrieked the dressmaker, "Never! The dress would be crushed. You must walk."

I hope it rains, thought Grace, crossing her fingers under the l-o-n-g gold sleeves. *If it rains, the* TOURNAMENT *might be cancelled.*

It did not rain.

The day of the TOURNAMENT dawned as bright and shiny as the golden dress.

The castle buzzed like a beehive. People swarmed into the gardens, dancers swirled around maypoles and knights in gleaming suits of armour CLANKED across the lawns.

The king flung back the doors of the castle and the cheering began.

"All hail the king," cried the crowd. "Hooray for Princess Grace."

Grace was shaking like royal jelly.

"I will not stumble," she murmured, walking slowly down the palace steps. "If I do not stumble, I will not . . .

FALL!

SPLAT!

Grace landed flat on her face, with the dress caught around the heel of her shoe.

The crowd gasped. Some people giggled.

"Whoops-a-daisy, Princess," a floppy-hatted jester said with a laugh.

Grace looked up at her father. His face was as **DARK** as thunder. He sighed, "Why can't you be more careful?"

Grace **struggled** to her feet, hitched up the dress and ran. Tears were streaming down her face. She hurtled around the corner of the castle, desperate to hide her shame.

"Why am I always so clumsy?" she wailed.

She **stumbled** into a field of tents where the knights were getting ready for the **TOURNAMENT**. Horses were tethered, saddles were being polished and suits of armour hung like laundry from the trees.

The knights were so busy with their preparations that they did not notice the sobbing *princess* **blundering** between the tents.

And *Grace* did not notice the sharp lance lying on the ground. The pointed end of the weapon caught in the l-o-n-g fabric of her dress.

R-r-r-r-i-p! *Grace* was still running when she heard the sound.

She looked around to see a glimmering gold train – as l-o-n-g as a cathedral aisle – lying on the ground.

Grace blushed as red as a raspberry. She was standing in nothing but her underwear, and the golden dress was ripped in half.

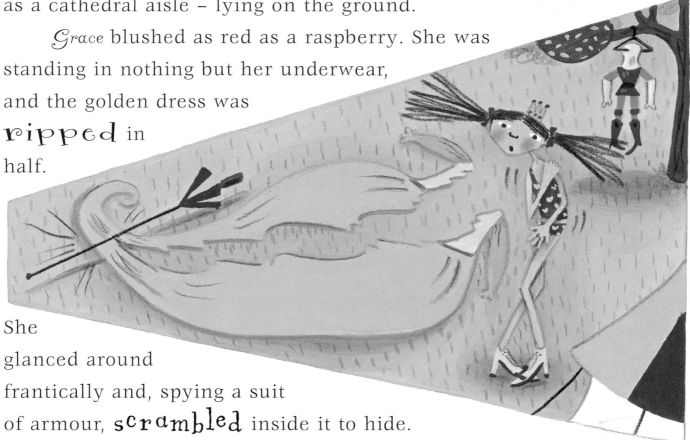

She glanced around frantically and, spying a suit of armour, scrambled inside it to hide.

At that moment, a fierce-looking squire with an ENORMOUS red moustache strode out of the nearest tent. He picked *Grace* up as if she and the armour weighed no more than a thimble and plonked her on a fine grey horse.

"GET GOING, SIR KNIGHT," he bellowed. "The contest is about to begin."

"B-but," mumbled Grace through the visor of her helmet.

"NO TIME TO ARGUE," snapped the squire. He threw her the lance and slapped the horse soundly on the rump. "Knock 'em down, Sir Knight. Knock 'em down."

"Whatever do you mean?" squealed Grace as the horse reared up and galloped towards the joust.

It soon became obvious what he had meant. *Grace* had to wield the great lance and **knock** other knights off their horses. She had to **knock** them off first, before they could unbalance her.

But *Grace* was good at **knocking** things down . . . very good! Knight after knight after knight **tumbled** and **fell** to the ground!

The crowd **leaped** to their feet and **cheered** for the slender rider on the fine grey horse.

"How brave he is," they whooped. "How well he knocks the others down."

Safe inside her armour, *Grace* did feel brave. She felt **STRONG** and fearless as her l-o-n-g legs gripped the saddle and her arms waved the lance in the air.

"Who's clumsy now?" she said and grinned. Then she knocked the last and fastest of the knights – CRASH! – to the ground.

A minstrel blew on his trumpet.

"THE CONTEST IS WON!" cried the fierce-looking squire.

"**Where's the** *princess?*" barked the king. "She should present the handkerchief now."

With trembling fingers Grace lifted up her helmet . . . and dropped it by mistake. There was a terrible clatter and a THUMP as it landed on the king's foot.

The crowd gasped.

"It's Princess Grace!" they cried, and they clapped and cheered louder than ever.

Grace smiled shyly and bowed.

The king smiled too.

"CONGRATULATIONS," he said, smiling and rubbing his foot. "From this day forward you will be known as the most skilful . . . and princessy . . . of all my knights."

And so it was that the jousting princess lived HAPPILY EVER AFTER . . . and never stopped knocking things down!

The
Princess
Exchange

Anne Marie Ryan

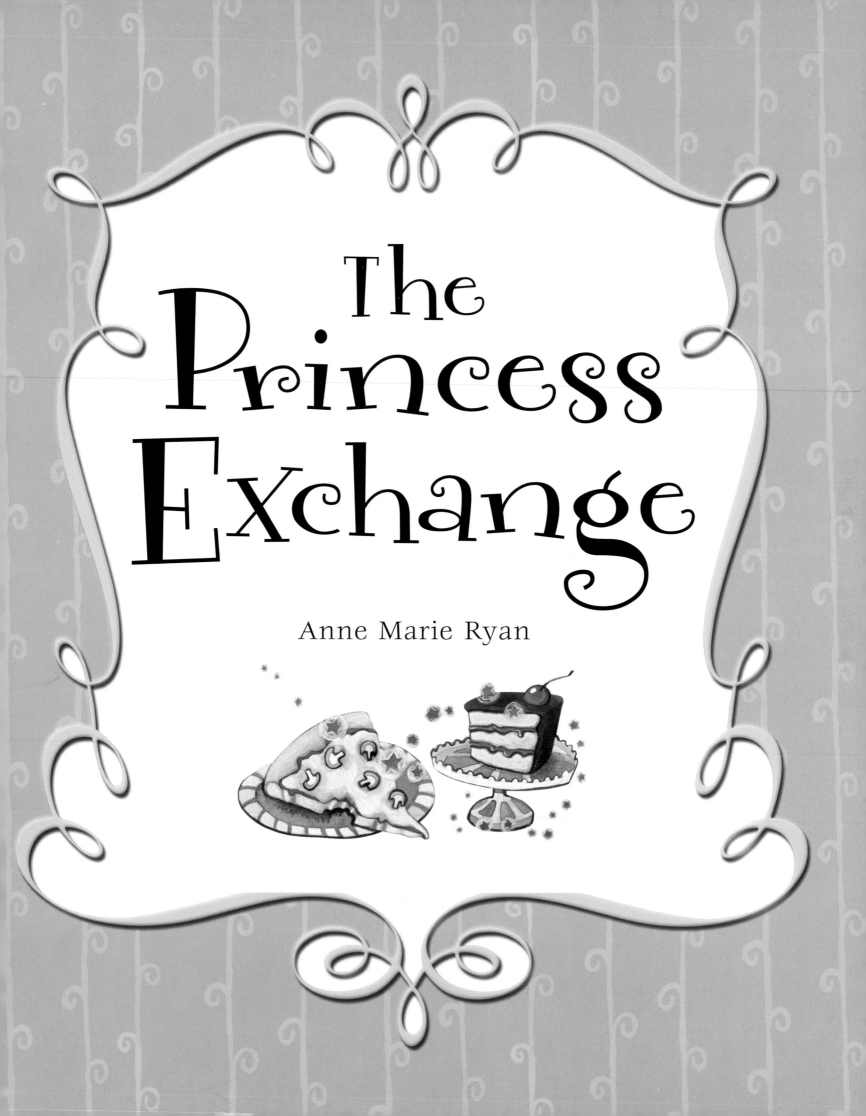

Once upon a time, there was a princess named Jane.

You'd probably never guess that she was a *princess*.

Her parents, King Brian and Queen Beatrice (or Bri and Bea as they liked to be called), were a very modern king and queen. They tried to lead ordinary lives like their subjects – they **never** wore their crowns when they went out and only let Princess Jane wear a tiara on very special occasions. But Princess Jane didn't want to be ordinary.

She dreamed of being a *fairy-tale princess* – the kind who lived in a *fancy palace*, married Prince Charming, and lived HAPPILY EVER AFTER.

After all, what was the point of being a *princess* if you didn't act like one? She didn't even sound like a *princess*, with a name like plain old Jane. How she longed to be named something truly regal, like *Arabella*, or *Clarissa*.

Now, Princess Jane and her parents lived in a perfectly comfortable little castle. They even had a few servants to help with the housekeeping. But their home was plain and pokey compared to the spectacular palaces pictured in the glossy pages of *Royalty Today* and *Smile & Wave*.

"I wish we could move," Princess Jane complained to King Bri as she flicked through her magazines. But the castle had been in King Bri's family for ages, and he thought it was just as cosy as could be.

"I wish you'd hold a ball," she begged Queen Bea. But instead the queen invited their subjects over for a barbecue in the ROYAL GARDENS.

"I wish we had a coach and six white horses," she grumbled when the footman drove her to school. But Princess Jane's parents thought that a minivan was more practical.

Though Bri and Bea didn't follow most ROYAL TRADITIONS, they had made one exception when their daughter was born. Princess Jane didn't just have a godmother – she had a *fairy godmother*.

24

One night, as
she got ready for bed,
Princess Jane heard a
POP – and out of nowhere her
fairy godmother appeared, raining a shower
of fairy dust all over the bedroom.

"You made three wishes, my dear," said Fairy
Godmother, coughing on the fairy dust. "So I've done my
best to grant them – I've arranged for a PRINCESS EXCHANGE.
Your third cousin twice removed, Princess Prunella, will be
coming here for the weekend. And you will go to stay with her
parents, King Leonard and Queen Lucinda, at Pepperhearst
Palace. I think you will find their style more to your liking."

Pepperhearst Palace! Princess Jane had admired pictures
of it in her magazines. "Thank you, Fairy Godmother," she
cried. "You're the best!"

With a flourish of her wand, Fairy Godmother disappeared
as suddenly as she had arrived, and Princess Jane went
to sleep with a smile on her face. The next morning
she woke to the sound of a trumpet fanfare.
Outside the castle stood a glittering golden
coach drawn by six white stallions. They
were tossing their manes and pawing
the ground impatiently. Princess
Jane kissed King Bri and
Queen Bea goodbye and
jumped into the coach.

25

The journey to *Pepperhearst Palace* was l-o-n-g and uncomfortable.

The carriage **shook** every time it went over a **bump**, so Princess Jane's bottom ached. The white stallions certainly looked impressive, but they were a bit **smelly** and kept flicking flies inside the coach with their tails. But at long last, *Pepperhearst Palace's* magnificent marble turrets **rose** in the distance.

King Leonard and Queen Lucinda received her in the throne room. "You'll want to change into something less comfortable," said the queen, giving Princess Jane's t-shirt and jeans a disapproving look. "One of the rules we have here at *Pepperhearst Palace* is that **PRINCESSES MUST WEAR THEIR TIARAS AT ALL TIMES.**"

Princess Jane eagerly changed into one of *Princess Prunella's* gowns – a flowing, sequinned confection with layer upon layer of skirts. Admiring herself in the mirror, she perched a sparkling **tiara** on top of her head. Finally, she looked like a real *princess*!

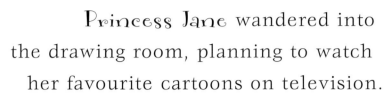

Princess Jane wandered into the drawing room, planning to watch her favourite cartoons on television. **"NO TIME FOR THAT COMMON NONSENSE,"** scolded Queen Lucinda. "Our *Prunella* spends her Saturday mornings at deportment class, followed by elocution lessons and ballroom-dance instruction."

By the end of the day, Princess Jane's head hurt from all of the lessons – and from a too-tight tiara. She was allowed to play in the palace grounds for one hour, but she kept tripping on her long skirts and couldn't climb trees in her dainty slippers.

That evening, King Leonard and Queen Lucinda held a **SPLENDID BALL** in honour of Princess Jane. After dancing for hours, Princess Jane had worked up an appetite. The banquet table overflowed with *fancy* morsels, but Princess Jane couldn't find a thing she wanted to eat. The caviar tasted like sweaty gym socks. The foie gras was too slimy. And the snails in garlic sauce just turned her tummy. "I wish they had some pizza and mint chocolate-chip ice cream," muttered Princess Jane. (That's what they always ate on Saturday nights back at her castle.)

When the clock struck midnight, a hungry and weary Princess Jane headed to bed. It was such a relief to take off her **pinching** tiara and **scratchy** ballgown. She climbed into bed, but couldn't fall asleep. It was just too **cold**. Her magazines never mentioned that big, marble palaces tended to be quite **chilly**. Princess Jane shivered and thought of her warm and cosy bedroom at home. **"I wish I was in my own bed,"** she whispered through **chattering** teeth.

"You look as though you haven't slept a wink," said Queen Lucinda at breakfast. "I hope *Princess Prunella* didn't leave a pea under her mattress as a prank. Look sharp – it's time for the ROYAL PROCESSION."

King Leonard, Queen Lucinda and Princess Jane squeezed into the golden coach and paraded through the streets all morning long.

"Smile and wave, smile and wave," ordered Queen Lucinda. Princess Jane's arm ached and her cheeks were sore from forcing a smile.

Through the coach's window, she could see other children playing hide-and-seek and riding bikes and chasing balls. If only she could get out and join them! But Queen Lucinda didn't allow *princesses* to mix with common children.

"Oh, how I wish I could go home!" Princess Jane wailed.

POP! As soon as she uttered the third wish, her *fairy godmother* appeared, filling the golden coach with a cloud of magical dust.

"But my dear, I thought *Pepperhearst Palace* was everything you ever wanted," said *Fairy Godmother*.

"It was," wept Princess Jane. "But there's no point acting like a *princess* if ordinary people have more fun."

(Which, of course, was what her parents had been telling her for years.)

And with a wave of *Fairy Godmother's* wand, Princess Jane was back home – just in time to join King Bri and Queen Bea for a walk through the park, where she played on the swings with the other children and got ice cream for a special treat.

31

"It's so good to be home," said Princess Jane happily, licking a cone of mint chocolate-chip.

"It's wonderful to have you back, darling," said Queen Bea. "That *Princess Prunella* was a bit too stuffy for us."

From that day on, Princess Jane was happy to be just plain old Jane. She sometimes dusted off her tiara and wore it to birthday parties or royal barbecues, but most of the time you'd probably never guess that she was a *princess*. And that was how she liked it.

The Princess and the P.E.

Angela Kanter

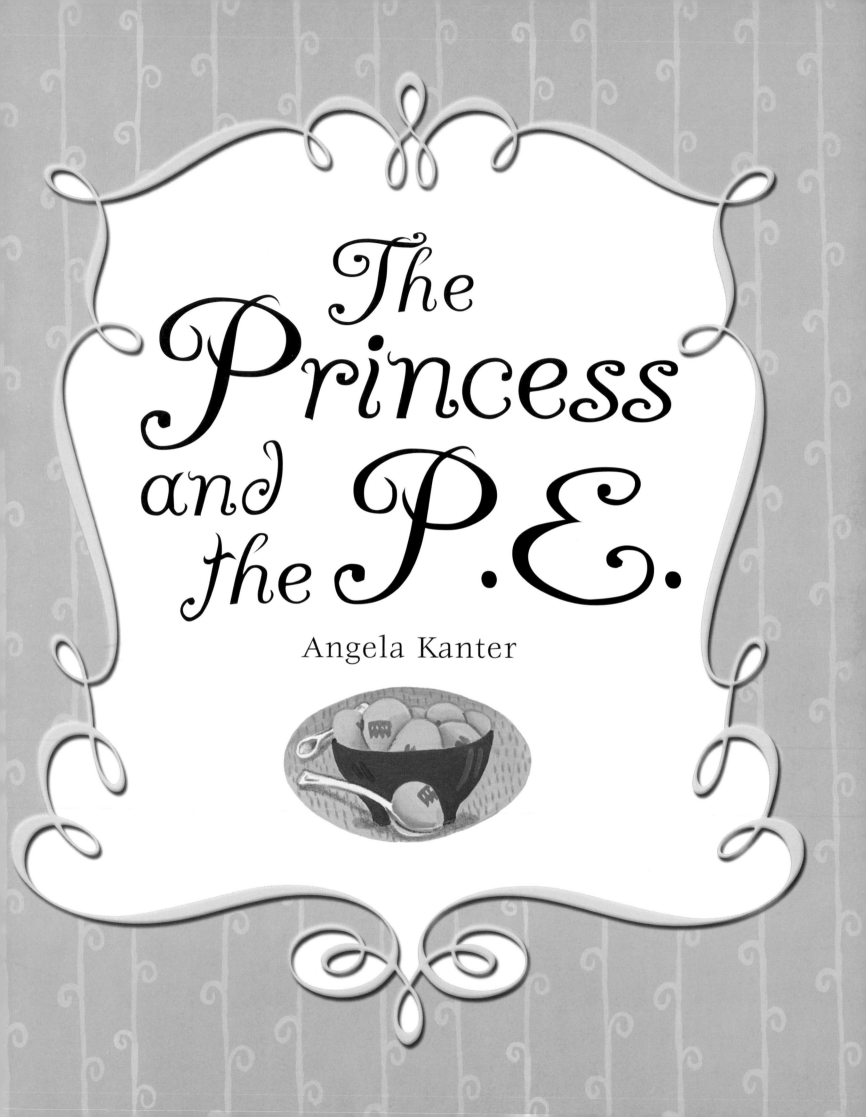

Princess Wendy was Crying.

It was SPORTS DAY soon at

Porlinda Perfect's School for princes and princesses and Princess Wendy was hopeless at sports.

There were two teams – **princes** and *princesses* – and the **princes'** team always won. And everybody said it was *Princess Wendy's* fault. She couldn't **run *fast***, or **ju**m**p HIGH**, or **catch a ball** like the other *princesses*.

"**Weed**y **Wend**y! You're the only bad one on the *princesses'* team," moaned horrible *Princess Eglantina*. It was all right for her, thought *Wendy. Princess Eglantina's fairy godmother* had given her a **leg-stre-e-e-tching** spell at birth – and now she could **run** and **ju**m**p** like a kangaroo.

"If it wasn't for you, we would win everything," whinged *Princess Viola*. It was all right for her, too. Her *fairy godmother* had given *Princess Viola* extra-bendy fingers that could **stre-e-e-tch** right around the field, so she could always **catch** any ball when it was thrown to her.

But what special powers had *Princess Wendy* been given? Only one. The ability to talk to **frogs**.

So that's why *Princess Wendy* was sitting by the school pond, crying, instead of changing into her shorts and t-shirt and going down to the sports field to practise with the rest of her class.

Suddenly, there was an ear-piercing whistle and a frog came bounding out of the water.

"What's up? What's up?" asked the frog briskly.

"All the other *princesses* in my class hate me," said *Princess Wendy*. "It's my fault we're not going to beat the **princes**' team on SPORTS DAY. I'm rubbish at sports. I can't even keep the golden egg on my spoon in the golden-goose race."

A big tear trickled down her cheek.

The frog flicked out his tongue and licked it off.

That made *Princess Wendy* giggle.

"Now, now!" said the frog. "Pay attention." And he blew his whistle again. *Princess Wendy* nearly fell in the pond with the shock.

"Please don't blow that thing," she begged.

"I will teach you how to jump and run," said the frog, taking no notice. "And we'll teach those other silly *princesses* a lesson, too. Now look. Follow me. Imagine you're jumping for something you really like to eat. A big fat fly, perhaps?"

"A chocolate éclair," said *Princess Wendy* firmly. And she tried to imagine it hanging there in the air.

The frog blew his whistle and she jumped so HIGH she could have snatched a chocolate éclair from the treetops.

"I said not to blow that thing!" said *Princess Wendy*, when she'd recovered.

"That was a jolly good jump," said the frog, ignoring her complaint. "Now – let's do some running. Imagine you're chasing something you really, really want. A delicious worm, perhaps."

"Pair of shoes," said *Princess Wendy*, breathlessly. "Silver ones, with roses on the front."

"If you must," said the frog. And he blew his whistle. *Princess Wendy* shot across the field, faster than – well, faster than a prince on SPORTS DAY. Finally, the frog showed her a special sticky leaf that she could rub on her hands to help her catch a ball.

"I could teach you to catch flies on your tongue as well, if you like," said the frog.

"No thanks," said *Princess Wendy*, trying to sound grateful. "I think I know enough now."

"Well, you're all ready for SPORTS DAY," said the frog. "I hope you win."

"Oh, thank you," said *Princess Wendy*. "But what about teaching the other *princesses* a lesson?"

"Oh, don't worry – just wait and see what happens," said the **frog**.

Princess Wendy walked back to the sports field.

"Ooh look – it's **Weedy Wendy!**" screeched *Princess Viola*.

"Come on, **Weedy**," called *Princess Eglantina*. "Come and help us lose again."

The **princes** were singing:

Princesses are silly,
Feeble and frilly!
Their clothes are far too pink,
And running makes them STINK!

And lots more verses that were much too rude to repeat.

But when the sports started, the **princes** were astonished. None of them could jump as HIGH as *Princess Wendy*. Or **run** as *fast*. Or catch the ball so many times. They just couldn't understand it. And for some reason, every time a race started, they seemed to hear this **ENORMOUS**, ear-splitting whistle. It really put the **princes** off.

At the end of SPORTS DAY, the *princesses'* team had a hundred points and the **princes** had no points at all.

"Well done!" said the other *princesses*, patting *Wendy* on the back. "You're our best friend, *Wendy*."

But *Wendy* wasn't fooled. She knew that the other *princesses* didn't really like her. They just wanted to win the SPORTS DAY.

The boys were speechless. Covered in mud and sweat, they didn't even have the heart to steal the girls' crowns while they were in the showers.

Porlinda Perfect walked on to the sports field, to present the golden cup to the winners.

"Who will collect the cup on behalf of the *Princesses*?" she asked.

Wendy wondered if the other *princesses* would choose her to collect the cup and get her picture taken by the photographer from the *Royal Report* newspaper. But *Princess Eglantina* and *Princess Viola* and all the other *princesses* started pushing forward. They wanted to be famous. They had forgotten all about *Princess Wendy*.

Just then, a **frog** croaked from some nearby bushes.

To the other *princesses*, it sounded just like, "Aark aark," but *Princess Wendy* knew that the **frog** was saying, "Hey, *Wendy* – it's me. Aren't you going to help me teach those *princesses* a lesson now?"

42

Wendy went over to the **frog**. She recognized him at once by the whistle he was wearing around his neck.

"Oh, thank you so much for helping me to do all that **jumping** and **running** and **catching**," said *Wendy*. "But it's OK. You don't have to punish the other *princesses*. I don't really mind about them. At least I'm good at sports now."

But really she was sad, because she still didn't have any proper friends.

The **frog** looked at her with big, sorrowful eyes.

"I'll be your best friend, *Wendy* – just **kiss** me," he said.

So *Wendy* bent down and **kissed** the **frog**. She didn't really fancy it, but after all he had been very kind to her – and he didn't really have more **warts** on his face than *Princess Viola*. Of course, the **frog** immediately turned into a **prince**.

"Ah, *Wendy*," said the **frog-prince**. "Think how jealous all the other *princesses* will be now, when you walk away with your handsome **prince** into the sunset."

43

Wendy looked at the **frog-prince**. He was wearing sports kit and he was very muddy and sweaty. He smelt really bad – which was fair enough for a **frog** in a pond, but not so good for a **prince**. She'd liked him better when he was a **frog**.

The **frog-prince** reached out to hug *Princess Wendy* with his sweaty, slimy arms.

Luckily, she now knew how to **run** very *fast*.

Sleepy
Beauty

William Bedford

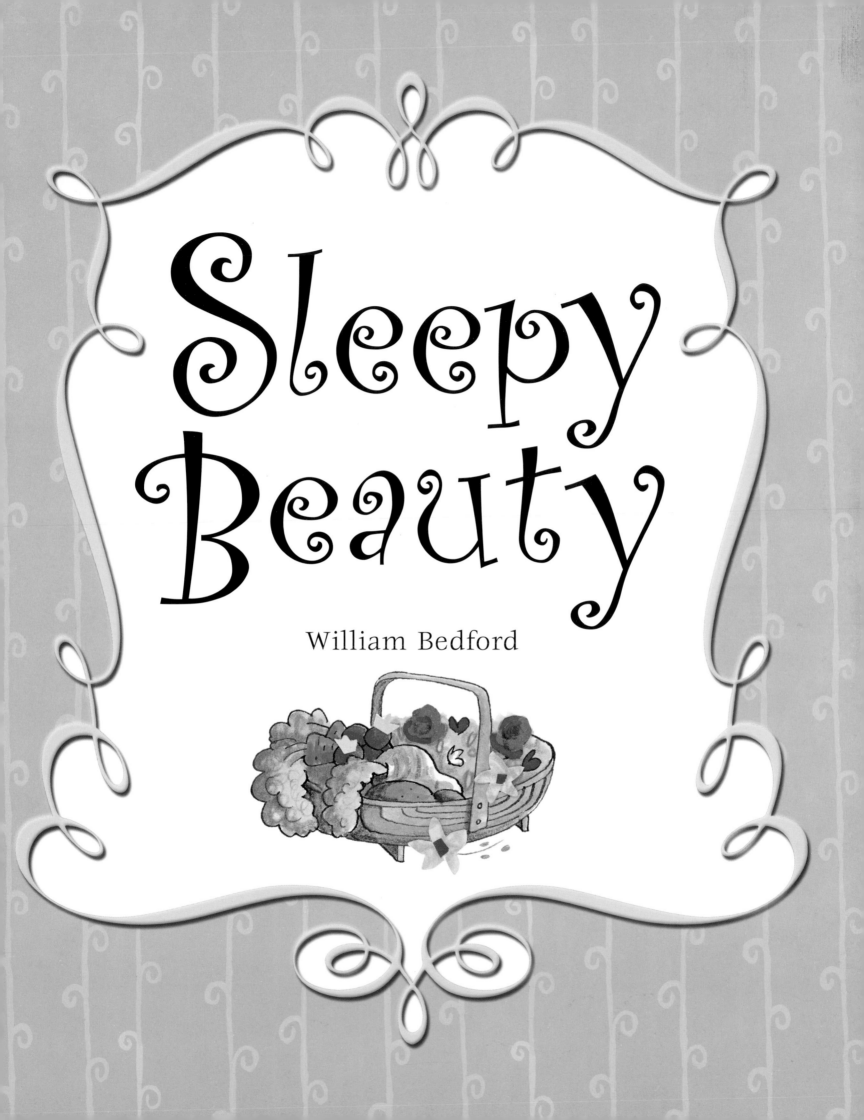

Sleepy Beauty loved to sleep.

She *snoozed* in the bathtub and swallowed a mouthful of bubbles.
She **dozed** during a really exciting chapter of *Royal Romances*.
She *napped* when the king was giving out prizes on SPORTS DAY.

Sleepy Beauty was the most *slumbery*, **drowsy**, *daydreamy* Sleepy Beauty anybody had ever known, and when she blushed her pink blush and lowered her blue eyes, everybody said, "Ahhh," and told her to go and have forty winks.

But the king was tired of seeing his daughter *snoozing* all the time. "What is the matter with my daughter?" he demanded. "Send for the ROYAL DOCTORS."

"Make her *sleep* in a bed of nettles and walk without shoes," said the first ROYAL DOCTOR.

"Make her drink cold water and keep her bedroom windows open," said the second ROYAL DOCTOR.

"Let her go to *sleep* and then shout 'BOO' very loudly every time she does," said the third ROYAL DOCTOR.

"Give me patience!" the king said impatiently.

He had heard all these medical opinions before. They never did any good. They just gave *Sleepy Beauty* a rash. "I don't know why I bother," muttered the king.

Then one day, a very old ROYAL DOCTOR hobbled up to the throne and bowed. He bowed and stayed bowed. It was several minutes before anybody noticed that he was stuck.

"Oh, do lift him up," the king said and sighed wearily. "What on earth are you doing out of bed?" he asked when the ROYAL DOCTOR was standing upright again.

"I think I know why *Sleepy Beauty* is so *catnappy* and dozy," the ROYAL DOCTOR said. "I remembered last night. The year the *princess* was born, when I was the king's favourite ..."

"This isn't going to take forever, is it?" the king said with a frown.

"...a **wicked witch** was here in the ROYAL PALACE," the old doctor went on without answering. He was quite deaf, you see, so he could ignore what the king said without appearing rude and losing his head, which can happen with angry kings.

48

"Actually, she wasn't that wicked," the ROYAL DOCTOR added with a shrug. "She was a nursery maid with a short temper. She definitely wanted to be a witch, but she kept failing her Spelling Tests, and they threw her out of Witch School."

"WHAT DID SHE DO?" the king yelled at the ROYAL DOCTOR.

"One day, she lost her temper and she cast a spell," the ROYAL DOCTOR continued. "I heard her say to the *princess*, 'You are so dozy that you should *sleep* for a hundred years.'

Then she should have said the part about eye of newt and toe of frog, but she forgot, and ran away. She's never been seen since."

The king turned white. He breathed heavily and closed his eyes. He took off his crown and polished it on his robe, which is what he always did when he was upset.

"So the spell didn't work," the ROYAL DOCTOR explained. "No eye of newt and toe of frog, so no spell. Just sort of half a spell. Sleepy Beauty instead of *Sleeping Beauty*, if you get the idea."

49

By the time the king had finished polishing his crown, the ROYAL DOCTOR had gone back to bed. The ROYAL POET stepped forward. "My king," he said, in that pompous voice poets always use. "I know the old story. I know the way the tale ends."

"Do you?" growled the king, in a voice that hinted that he would like to see the ROYAL POET'S tale end, and not HAPPILY EVER AFTER. "You'd better tell us then, as that's what you're paid for."

"The tale ends," said the poet, "when a prince hacks his way through the garden, kisses the *princess*, and wakes her up from her *sleepiness*. It's only half a spell, so you probably won't even need a prince. A poet would do just as well."

The king turned red this time, like a tomato. "Nobody's going to hack through my garden," he yelled from the throne. "Nobody's going to kiss this *princess* – oh no, not even a ROYAL POET. So you'd better go away and think of a better ending than that!"

50

So things went on as before. Sleepy Beauty slumbered and **nodded off**, but she smiled so sweetly when she was *asleep*, and she smiled so sweetly when she was awake, that EVERYBODY *fell in love* with her.

But the news got out. The ROYAL POET was not good at keeping his mouth shut. He told everybody the secret to ending Sleepy Beauty's *sleepiness*. And as the rumours spread, young **princes** began to gather at the borders.

One was found in the rose garden, hacking down the roses.

"BOIL HIM IN BEER," yelled the king, and the guards quickly took him to the border and threw him back.

One of them was found in the orchard, sawing branches off the apple trees.

"DROP HIM IN THE DUNGEON," the king bellowed, and the guards wrapped him up in brown paper, covered him in stamps and sent him back to his parents.

One of them was caught in the vegetable garden, digging up all the carrots and turnips.

"FLOAT HIM IN THE MOAT," the king shouted,

and the guards pushed him into a wheelbarrow and trundled him down to the docks and onto the first ship sailing back to his own country.

Sleepy Beauty thought that all of this was very funny. "These men," she said and giggled, raising her eyebrows and blushing. "The things they will do for exercise."

"It isn't exercise they want," the king growled.

The ROYAL GARDENS were a mess. All the gardeners had run away. They were sick of being attacked by princes.

"We need a new gardener," the king said.

So they advertised in the village, and soon a young man came by with his gardening tools.

Sleepy Beauty had never seen anyone so handsome. He was tanned by the sun and wore a single gold earring. His old boots were red leather and polished to a fine shine. He had very blue eyes, which she couldn't stop looking into. His name was Tom.

Tom soon planted new roses and repaired the damage to the apple trees. He planted fresh vegetables and took the carrots and turnips to the kitchens.

He sang while he worked and *Sleepy Beauty* got in the way, *falling asleep*, **tripping** over forks and spades, **tearing** her dress and filling her hair with straw. She hadn't enjoyed herself so much in her whole life.

It took them a week to put the gardens straight. "Do you want some lemonade?" she asked when they were finished.

"Thank you," Tom said.

So they sat together drinking lemonade and playing **KINGS &
QUEENS**, a very old card game. When *Sleepy Beauty* won the tenth game, she was so excited that she flung her arms around the young man's neck and *kissed* him.

And just like that the *sleepy* feeling left her. It simply disappeared. It **flew** away above the apple trees, and never came back.

"That's *amazing*," Sleepy Beauty said.

"What do you mean?" asked Tom, feeling slightly puzzled. He was used to dealing with flowers and vegetables, you see, not *girls*. But he was willing to learn.

By the time the king arrived home from his **HOW TO GET RID OF DOCTORS** lesson, Sleepy Beauty and Tom had fallen in love, and the king was so pleased that Sleepy Beauty had lost all of her *sleepiness* that he said they could get married, as long as Tom agreed to look after the **ROYAL GARDENS**.

So they did, and everybody lived **HAPPILY EVER AFTER**.

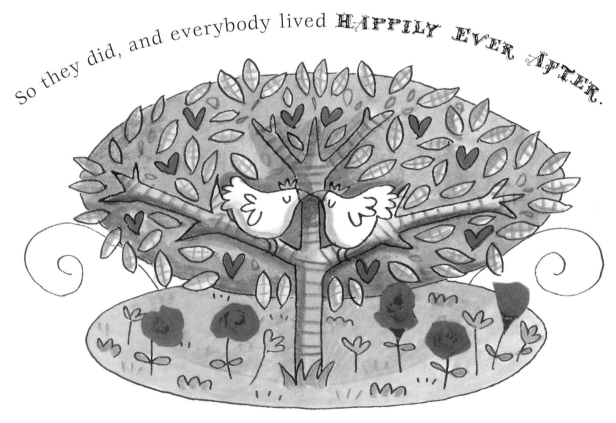

Double Dragons

Enid Richemont

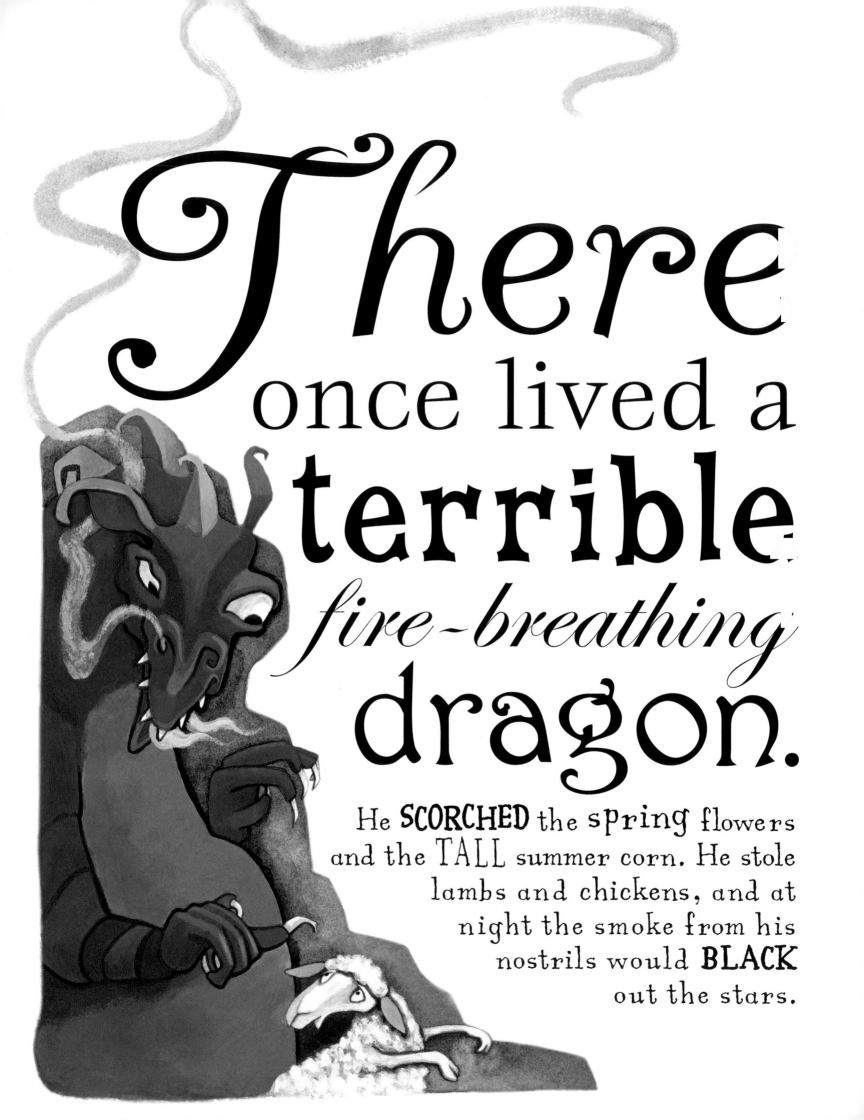

There once lived a terrible fire-breathing dragon.

He **SCORCHED** the spring flowers and the TALL summer corn. He stole lambs and chickens, and at night the smoke from his nostrils would **BLACK** out the stars.

"Whoever kills the dragon," cried the king, "can marry my daughter."

But, one by one, the knights straggled back, sucking burned fingers and d-r-agging broken swords and battered shields.

Sometimes they didn't come back at all.

Then, deep inside his cave, the dragon would pat his scaly tummy.

"Roast lamb may be good," he sang, "but barbecued knight's got that little something . . ."

One day the dragon made a TERRIBLE demand.

"Send me your most *beautiful* maiden," he roared, "or I'll burn down your city."

"I'll go!" cried Princess Greta. "Anything to save me from marrying some boring old knight!"

"But you're not *beautiful*," said her brother.

"*Beauty*," said Greta, "is a matter of taste. And besides, that dragon needs to be sorted out."

"Girls can't fight dragons," argued the king.

"This one can," said Greta, and she packed a bag and leaped on a horse before anyone could stop her.

The **dragon's** trail was easy
to follow – a **SCORCHED** track across
the moor and through the forest.

Greta stopped to rest, tethering
her horse to a tree. Then, in the
distance, she noticed a pool.
"Just what I need," she said
and sighed.
She picked her way through
the bracken and found it –
a circle of deep water, like
a mirror. She saw her
plump pink cheeks,
and her sticking-out
ears in its clear surface.

It's a nice face, Greta thought as
she drank, *and I like it. And besides,
I've just had a brilliant idea.*

60

"Who are you?" roared the dragon when Greta arrived at his cave.

"You asked for a *beautiful* maiden," said Greta.

"I wanted blue eyes," grumbled the dragon, "and long golden hair."

"Who told you that was *beautiful*?" Greta asked.

"It's in my book," confessed the dragon, "under: *Maidens, beautiful.*"

"Then your book's out of date," said Greta. "Not like the other dragon's."

The dragon spat out BLASTS of *fire* and SMOKE.

"What other dragon?" he bellowed.

"The one I met near the forest," said Greta.

"There are no other dragons!" howled the dragon.

"Oh yes there are," said Greta. "And he was looking for a *beautiful* maiden too. But I told him I was booked." She wrinkled her nose. "Your breath stinks!" she complained. "It's all that rotten meat you keep eating. Nuts and berries would make you smell so much nicer."

"I'm not a vegetarian!" roared the dragon.

"But you could be," said Greta.

The dragon was puzzled.

"Aren't you scared of me?" he growled.

"Not as scared as I was of the other dragon," said Greta.

"I could **roast** you and EAT you," he threatened.

Greta shrugged. "The other dragon's *flames*," she said and sighed, "were like a volcano."

The **dragon** closed his eyes, but he couldn't sleep.

At dawn he **rose** into the **air** and flew out over the land.

At noon he came back. The sun was **high** in the sky and there wasn't a breath of wind.

"I saw no other **dragon**!" he thundered.

Greta climbed on to his back. "I'll show you," she said.

The **dragon** spread his wings.
Mmmm, I like **flying**, thought Greta.

"He's somewhere down here," she whispered, when she spotted the pool.

"I'll get him!" roared the **dragon**. "I'll STUFF his tail down his THROAT! I'll SCORCH holes in his wings!"

"*Shhh!*" Greta whispered. "He's bigger than you. Quick, swoop down! We'll surprise him."

They slithered through the bracken.

"There he is!" Greta cried, pointing at the dragon's reflection.

The dragon looked. He bristled with rage.

"This is WAR!" he bellowed, shooting out a tongue of yellow flames.

But the dragon in the pool simply shot out another.

"I'll SCRATCH your eyes out!" roared the dragon, and he reared up and lunged.

SPLASH!

The water bubbled and boiled.

The dragon's head **rose** up out of the pool.

"You tricked me, false maiden!" he roared.

He **rose** a second time.

"My *flames* have gone out!" he wailed. "Oh the shame of it!"

He **rose** for a third time.

"Help!" he spluttered. "Help!"

"No more stealing lambs and chickens?" demanded Greta. "Not to mention knights!"

The dragon shook his head miserably:

PLOOP – PLOP!

"But how can I trust you?" asked Greta.

"Dragon's honour," gasped the dragon.

So Greta found a stout stick and pulled him out.

The **dragon** lay, not moving. Greta pounded on his chest, but only **bubbles** came out. "I don't want you to be dead," she cried. "And I did like **flying**."

The **dragon** opened one eye. "I've lost my *flames*," he moaned. "You should have let me drown."

"Oh don't say that," said Greta. "I'm sure we can find a use for you."

A strange little procession made its way back to the city. Greta led on her horse, followed meekly by the **dragon**.

The king, the queen and Greta's brother were watching from the castle.

"She's tamed him!" cried the king.

"What a daughter!" cried the queen.

"What a sister!" cried her brother.

"Of course the dragon must be killed," declared the king.

"Why?" demanded Greta. "He's stopped breathing *fire*, and he's made a dragon's-honour promise to be good. In fact, he's become a vegetarian."

The dragon blushed pink. "Oh, the shame of it!" he groaned.

"And I've got an idea," said Greta. "Doesn't our kingdom need a public transportation system?"

They built the dragon a hangar on the city square.

DRAGON AIR

it said in big gold letters (it made him very proud). People bought tickets to fly to see faraway grannies and aunties.

The king made Greta the Royal Dragon Keeper, and every night, she and the dragon would go flying together under the stars.

Princess
Rose

Elaine Canham & Rose Canham

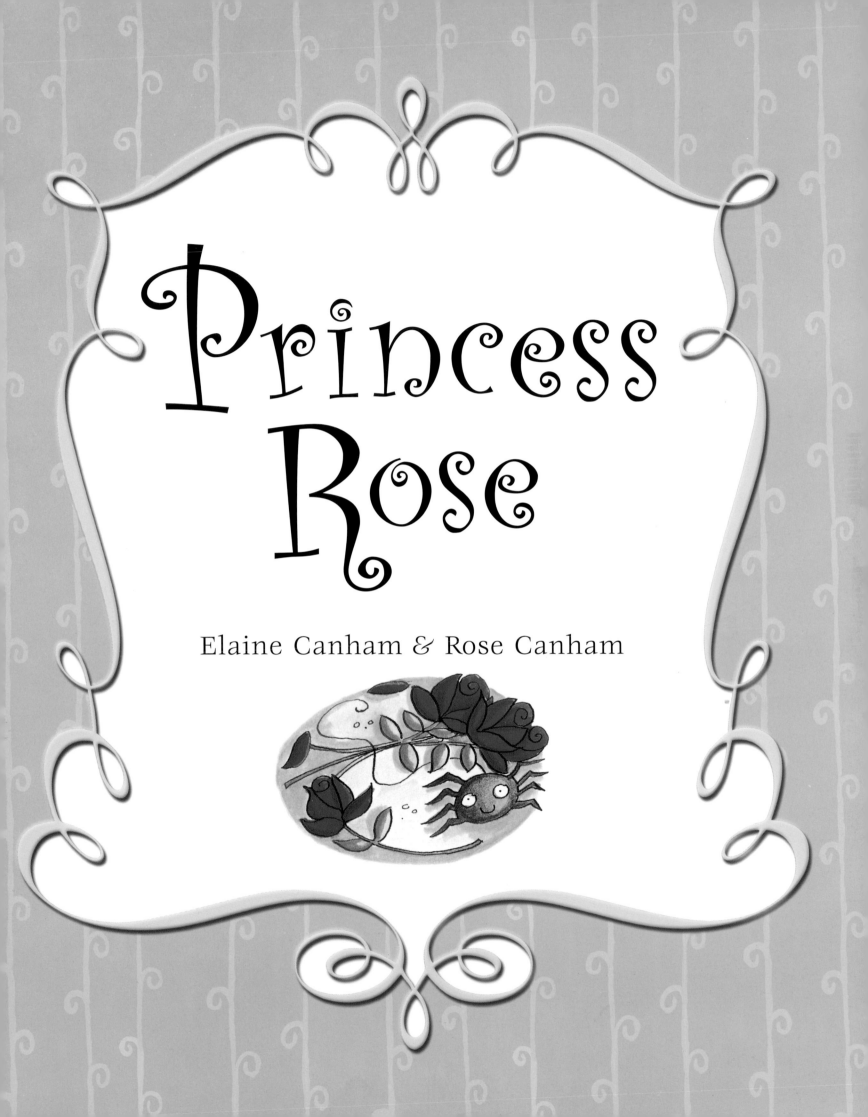

Once upon a time there was a princess named Rose.

She was kind and clever and BRAVE. She liked horses and spiders and chocolate, but she hated spelling and frogs and peas.

One day, she decided she wanted to marry a handsome **prince**, but there weren't any **princes** living nearby.

Her mother, the queen, said, "I did hear of one **prince** down south who is looking for a *princess*, but for some reason his mother insists on putting peas under all the mattresses."

"Ugh," said Princess Rose. "It's bad enough having peas on your plate, never mind all over your bed. He won't do at all."

Her father, the king, said, "I heard of a **prince** up north who was quite handsome before he got changed into a frog. You'd need to kiss him though, to get him back to normal."

"Yuck," said Princess Rose. "No way. He'll have to get somebody else."

Her little brother, Prince William, said, "Well, you're not marrying me. Girls are **AWFUL**."

"Get real," said Princess Rose, and she decided to put an ad in the paper.

WANTED:

NICE PRINCE. MUST HAVE GOOD MANNERS AND BE KIND TO ANIMALS. MUST LIKE CHOCOLATE.

But no one replied. "I can't keep waiting like this," she said and sighed. "I will just have to go and **find** a **prince**."

So she saddled up her horse and packed her lunchbox and off she went. She spent the whole afternoon looking for a **prince**, but she couldn't **find** one anywhere.

Then it got **dark**, so she had a sleepover at her friend *Rapunzel's* tower. "I wish I could go and look for a **prince**," *Rapunzel* said with a sigh. "But I've just got to wait here and let down my hair every time someone calls. I'm sure it's not good for my roots. I'd like to have short hair, and dye it blue."

"Never mind," said Rose. "I'm sure someone will be along soon to free you, and then you'll be able to get to a hairdresser."

The next day Rose said goodbye to *Rapunzel* and went on with her search. She went **up** hill and **down** dale and **over** yonder and **hither** and **thither**.

She was riding by a BIG bog when she heard someone shouting, "Help! Help!" So she got off her horse and went to look.

In the bog was a **prince** who had fallen off his horse. He was covered in **mud**.

"HANG ON!" shouted Princess Rose. "I'll have you out in two ticks." So she tied a rope to her horse and threw the other end to the **prince** and when he caught it she asked her horse very nicely to pull him out.

And when the **prince** rather **squelchily** stood before her, she said, "I'm looking for a **prince** to marry. You look nice. What do you think?"

But the **prince** replied, "I can't. I'm going to see another *princess* and I'm taking her a special gift of **chocolates**. I must get going, before they melt."

"Oh," said Princess Rose. "Bother."

The **prince** shrugged. "I must go, before I *fall in love* with you instead, which wouldn't be fair to the other one." And then he looked deep into her eyes and said *tenderly,* "Did you know you have a spider in your hair?" And he took it out and put it *gently* in a bush.

And then he got on his horse and rode off and they spent a l-o-n-g time waving goodbye to each other. When he finally disappeared over a hill, she got on her horse and went on looking for a **prince**, but in the whole afternoon she didn't see a single one.

75

That night she stayed with **The Three Bears**. "Oh, if it's **princes** you want," said **Papa Bear**, "I saw a few at Sleepy Beauty's castle yesterday trying to hack their way through the undergrowth."

"They're very silly," said **Mama Bear**. "I don't know why they just don't use a decent weedkiller and save themselves all that trouble."

"I want more porridge," said **Baby Bear**.

The next day Princess Rose went sadly home. "I did my best," she said to her mother and father. "But there are just no **princes** anywhere. I think I'll have a bath and put my nightie on and go to bed."

"Are you kidding?" said the king.

"Don't be silly," said the queen.

"There are **MILLIONS** of **princes** in the **THRONE ROOM**," said Prince William. "They've all come because of your ad. It's just taken them a while to get here."

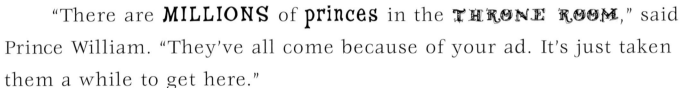

So Princess Rose ran to the THRONE ROOM and all the princes – there were 120 of them – immediately *fell in love* with her and got down on their knees and asked her to marry them. All at once.

The noise was INCREDIBLE.
"Goodness," said Princess Rose.
"That's me," said a voice. And one
of the **princes** stood up. "Prince
Goodness at your service."

It was the **prince** she had rescued from the bog. He bowed and, pausing only to rescue a small spider that was in danger of being stepped on, handed her a box of chocolates. Rose *fell in love* with him immediately, and they were married the next day and lived HAPPILY EVER AFTER.